There are a lot of stories about that creepy-looking mansion on the hill, but Danny Crowe is living one far creepier than anything he's heard. His adventurer Grandpa promised him they'd explore the mansion one day, but a freak accident killed his gramps and put that plan in the ground. Right? WRONG! Madame Leota, a ghost in a crystal ball, reached out to Danny from the mansion to deliver a message: his Grandpa's ghost is in the mansion, and needs his help!

Danny plucked up every bit of courage he had and set out for the mansion, learning from Madame Leota that the house is populated with retired ghosts. Most want to relax and enjoy their (after)lives, but a sinister spirit known only as the Captain has found a way to trap the ghosts inside. Only a living person can free the mansion and Grandpa's spirit, so Danny agrees to help. Now he just has to *remain living...*

Welcome, foolish mortals, to...

The Haunted Mansion

#2

Danny

Madame Leota

JOSHUA WILLIAMSON writer **JORGE COELHO** artist

JEAN-FRANCOIS BEAULIEU - colorist VC's JOE CARAMAGNA - letterer E. M. GIST - cover artist
BRIAN CROSBY - variant cover artist JOHN TYLER CHRISTOPHER - action figure variant cover artist

ANDY DIGENOVA, TOM MORRIS, JOSH SHIPLEY - Walt Disney Imagineers
EMILY SHAW & MARK BASSO - editors AXEL ALONSO - editor in chief
JOE QUESADA - chief creative officer DAN BUCKLEY - publisher

special thanks to DAVID GABRIEL, BRIAN CROSBY & CHRIS D'LANDO

ABDO Spotlight Disney KINGDOMS MARVEL

ABDOPUBLISHING.COM

Reinforced library bound edition published in 2017 by Spotlight,
a division of ABDO, PO Box 398166, Minneapolis, Minnesota 55439.
Spotlight produces high-quality reinforced library bound editions for
schools and libraries. Published by agreement with Marvel Characters, Inc.

Printed in the United States of America, North Mankato, Minnesota.
092016
012017

THIS BOOK CONTAINS
RECYCLED MATERIALS

marvelkids.com
© 2016 MARVEL

**Elements based on
The Haunted Mansion® attraction
© Disney.**

PUBLISHER'S CATALOGING IN PUBLICATION DATA

Names: Williamson, Joshua, author. | Coelho, Jorge ; Beaulieu, Jean-Francois,
    illustrators.
Title: The haunted mansion / writer: Joshua Williamson ; art: Jorge Coelho,
    Jean-Francois Beaulieu.
Description: Reinforced library bound edition. | Minneapolis, Minnesota : Spotlight,
    2017. | Series: Disney kingdoms : haunted mansion
Summary: When a ghostly woman appears to Danny urging him to come to the
    haunted mansion and help his dead grandpa's spirit, Danny enters the house
    and agrees to help the spirits trapped inside, that is if he can survive.
Identifiers: LCCN 2016949392 | ISBN 9781614795872 (v.1 ; lib. bdg.) | ISBN
    9781614795889 (v.2 ; lib. bdg.) | ISBN 9781614795896 (v.3 ; lib. bdg.) | ISBN
    9781614795902 (v.4 ; lib. bdg.) | ISBN 9781614795919 (v.5 ; lib. bdg.)
Subjects: LCSH: Apparitions--Juvenile fiction. | Haunted houses--Juvenile fiction. |
    Grandfathers--Juvenile fiction. | Survival--Juvenile fiction. | Graphic novels--
    Juvenile fiction.
Classification: DDC 741.5--dc23
LC record available at https://lccn.loc.gov/2016949392

Spotlight

A Division of ABDO
abdopublishing.com

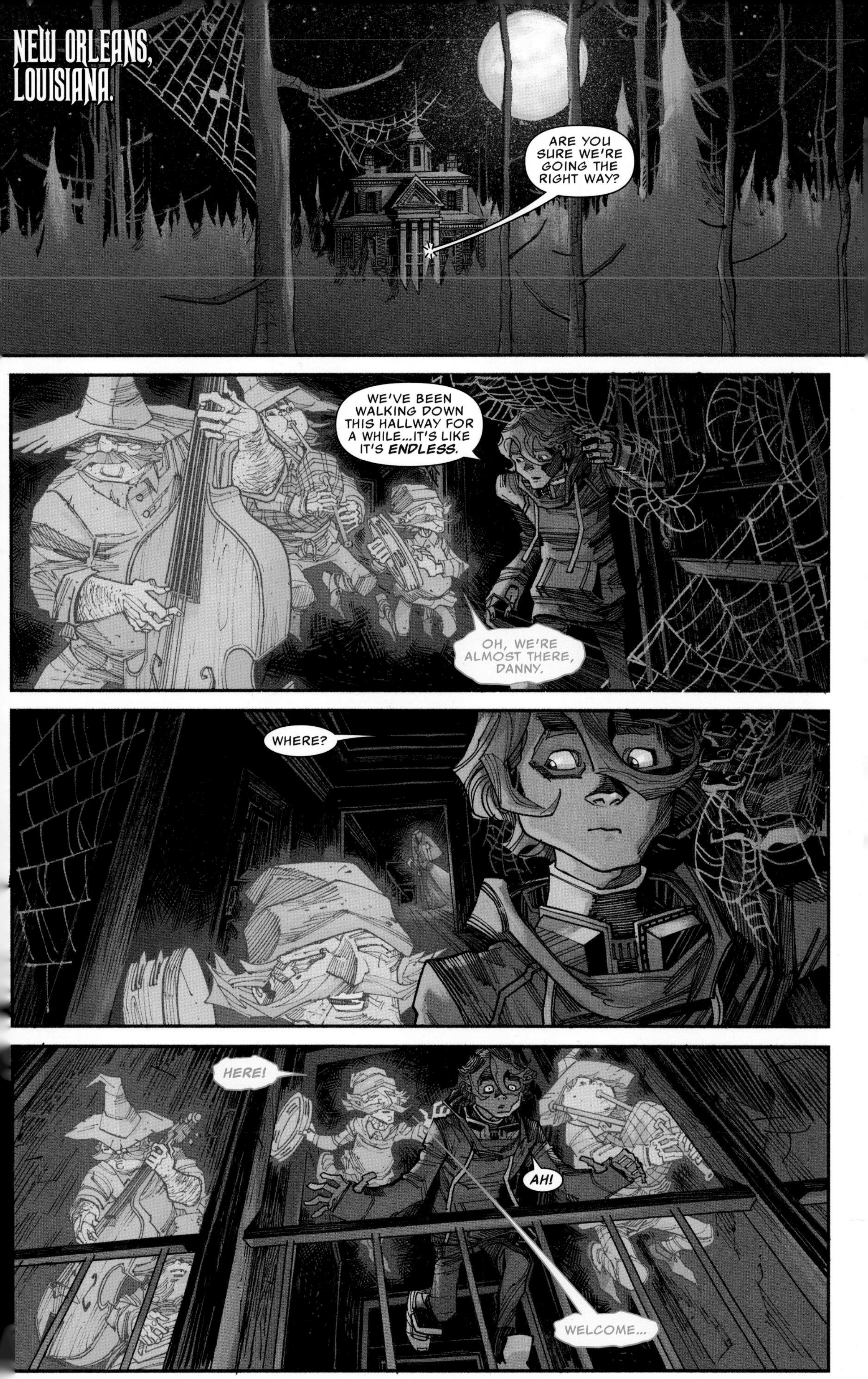
NEW ORLEANS, LOUISIANA.
ARE YOU SURE WE'RE GOING THE RIGHT WAY?
WE'VE BEEN WALKING DOWN THIS HALLWAY FOR A WHILE...IT'S LIKE IT'S ENDLESS.
OH, WE'RE ALMOST THERE, DANNY.
WHERE?
HERE!
AH!
WELCOME...

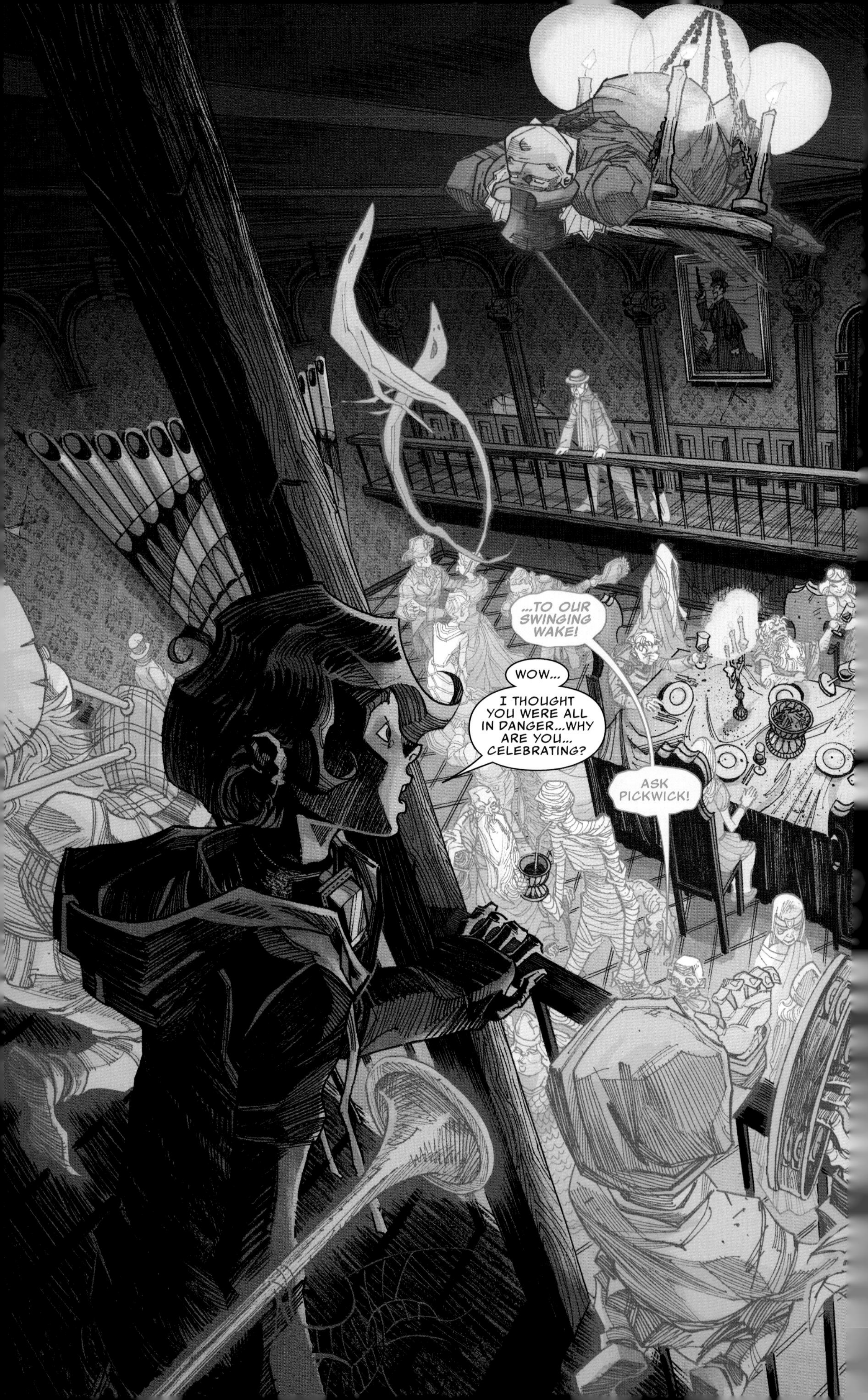
...TO OUR SWINGING WAKE!
WOW...
I THOUGHT YOU WERE ALL IN DANGER...WHY ARE YOU... CELEBRATING?
ASK PICKWICK!

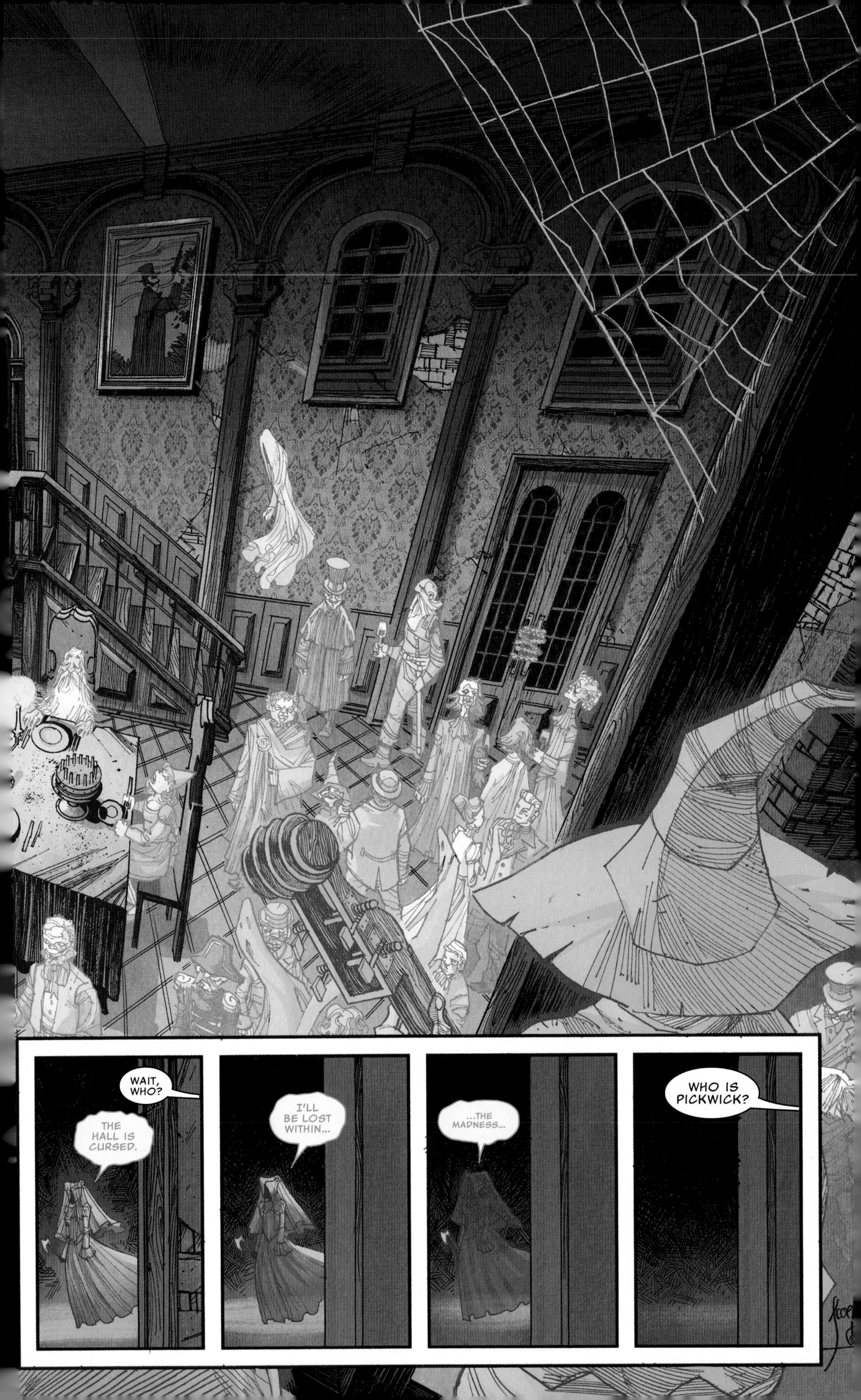
WAIT, WHO?
THE HALL IS CURSED.
I'LL BE LOST WITHIN...
...THE MADNESS...
WHO IS PICKWICK?

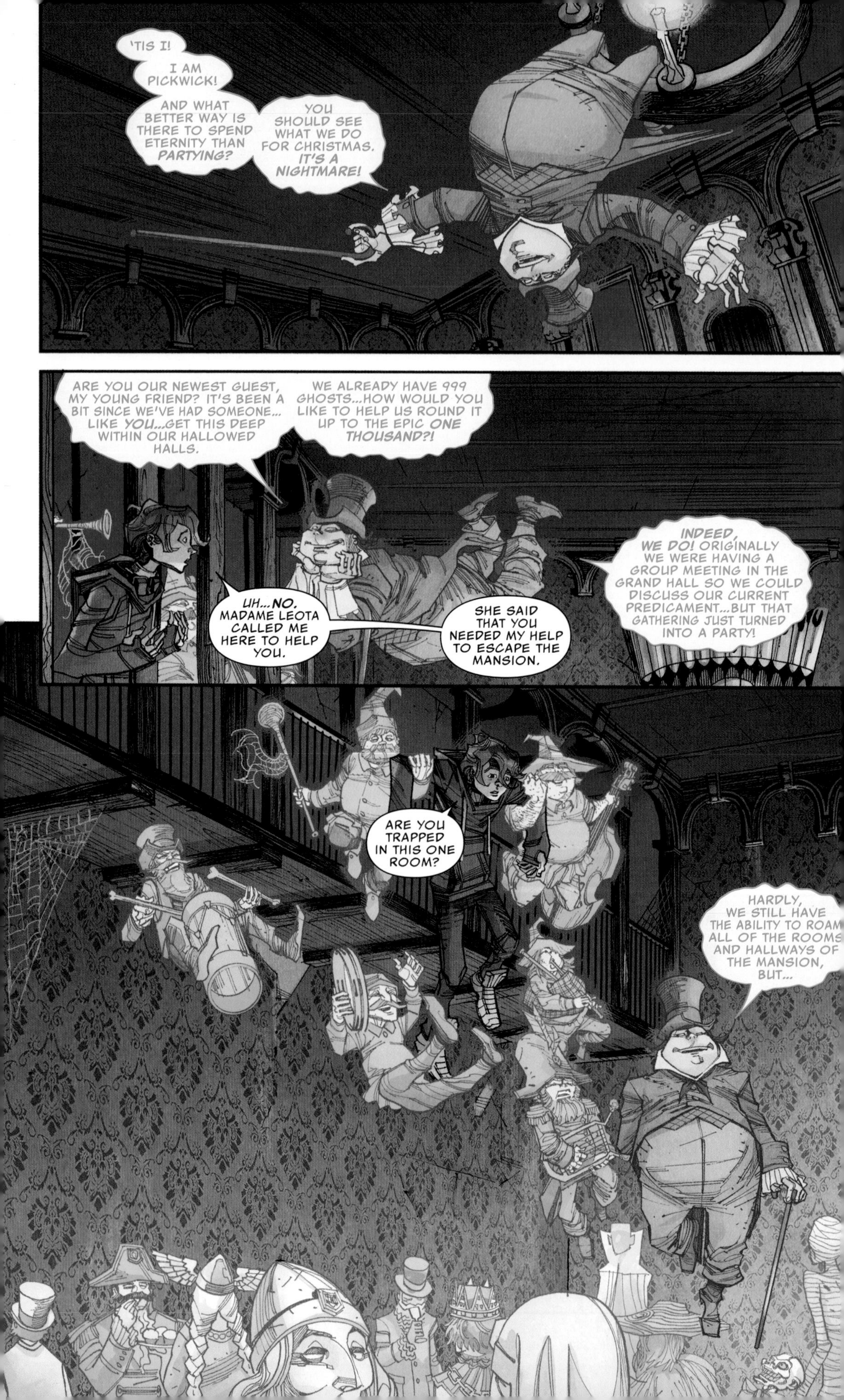
'TIS I!
I AM PICKWICK!
AND WHAT BETTER WAY IS THERE TO SPEND ETERNITY THAN PARTYING?
YOU SHOULD SEE WHAT WE DO FOR CHRISTMAS. IT'S A NIGHTMARE!
ARE YOU OUR NEWEST GUEST, MY YOUNG FRIEND? IT'S BEEN A BIT SINCE WE'VE HAD SOMEONE... LIKE YOU...GET THIS DEEP WITHIN OUR HALLOWED HALLS.
WE ALREADY HAVE 999 GHOSTS...HOW WOULD YOU LIKE TO HELP US ROUND IT UP TO THE EPIC ONE THOUSAND?!
UH...NO. MADAME LEOTA CALLED ME HERE TO HELP YOU.
SHE SAID THAT YOU NEEDED MY HELP TO ESCAPE THE MANSION.
INDEED, WE DO! ORIGINALLY WE WERE HAVING A GROUP MEETING IN THE GRAND HALL SO WE COULD DISCUSS OUR CURRENT PREDICAMENT...BUT THAT GATHERING JUST TURNED INTO A PARTY!
ARE YOU TRAPPED IN THIS ONE ROOM?
HARDLY, WE STILL HAVE THE ABILITY TO ROAM ALL OF THE ROOMS AND HALLWAYS OF THE MANSION, BUT...

SEE THESE DOORS? THEY *USED* TO BE ONE OF THE MAIN ENTRY POINTS FOR NEW SPIRITS TO JOIN OUR FESTIVITIES. BUT NOW, LIKE ALL THE DOORS AND WINDOWS...THEY HAVE BEEN *LOCKED*.

WE USED TO BE ABLE TO COME AND GO AS WE PLEASED. BUT THE *CAPTAIN* IS KEEPING US PRISONER IN THE MANSION.

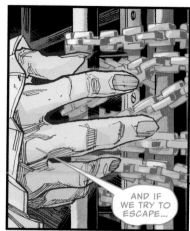

AND IF WE TRY TO ESCAPE...

WHOOSSHHH

ARE YOU OKAY?

BEEN A LONG TIME SINCE ANY OF US HAVE FELT *PAIN* LIKE THAT. ANY PAIN FOR THAT MATTER!

EVER SINCE *THE CAPTAIN'S* CURSE, WE HAVEN'T EXACTLY BEEN... RESTING IN PEACE.

BUT...

NO MATTER HOW MUCH WE... WANT...TO BE FREE...

...WE JUST CAN'T...

...LEAVE THE PARTY!

...WHAT WERE WE TALKING ABOUT?

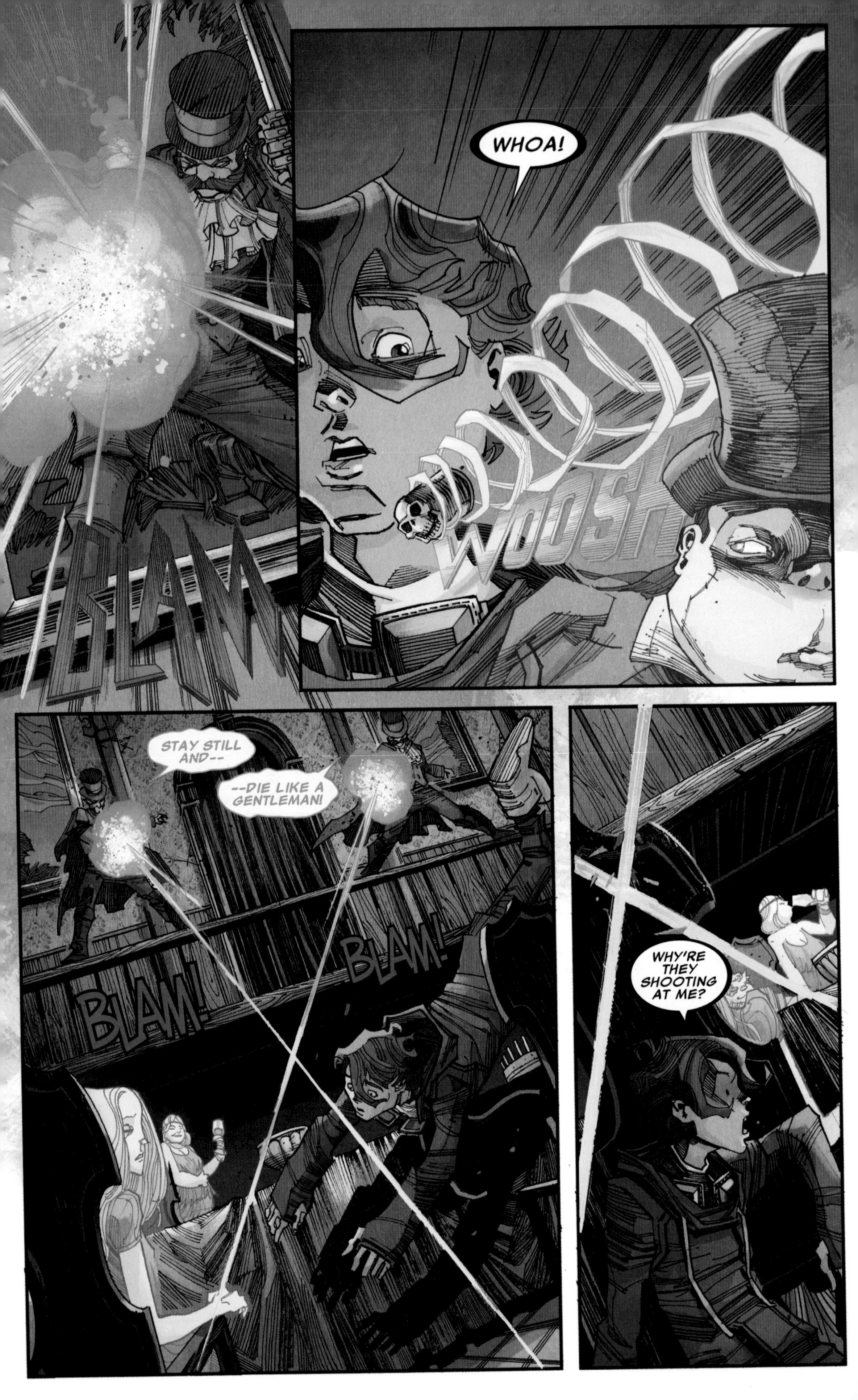
BLAM
WHOA!
WOOSH
STAY STILL AND--
--DIE LIKE A GENTLEMAN!
BLAM!
BLAM!
WHY'RE THEY SHOOTING AT ME?

DON'T WORRY, YOUNG MAN. THE DUELING GHOSTS ARE USING ENCHANTED CORPOREAL PISTOLS...SO THEY CAN'T *REALLY* HURT ANYTHING...UNLESS IT'S *ALIVE*, THAT IS.

HA HA HA HA HA HA HA HA HA HA

I AM ALIVE!

OH, THAT'S RIGHT.

YOU REALLY *SHOULD* BE A GHOST. IT WOULD BE SO MUCH EASIER FOR YOU IN THE MANSION IF YOU WERE--

BLAM!

--GET OUT OF HERE!

YOU'RE GOING TO RUIN THE PARTY!

DON'T MIND THEM... THEY'RE HORRIBLE SHOTS.

I THINK THE ONLY TIME THEY ACTUALLY HIT *ANYTHING* IS WHEN THEY HIT *EACH OTHER*.

THE DUELING GENTLEMEN GHOSTS WERE SOME OF THE FIRST TO FALL UNDER *THE CAPTAIN'S THRALL*.

SO HOW COME THE CAPTAIN CAN MESS WITH THE OTHER, UH... GHOSTS?

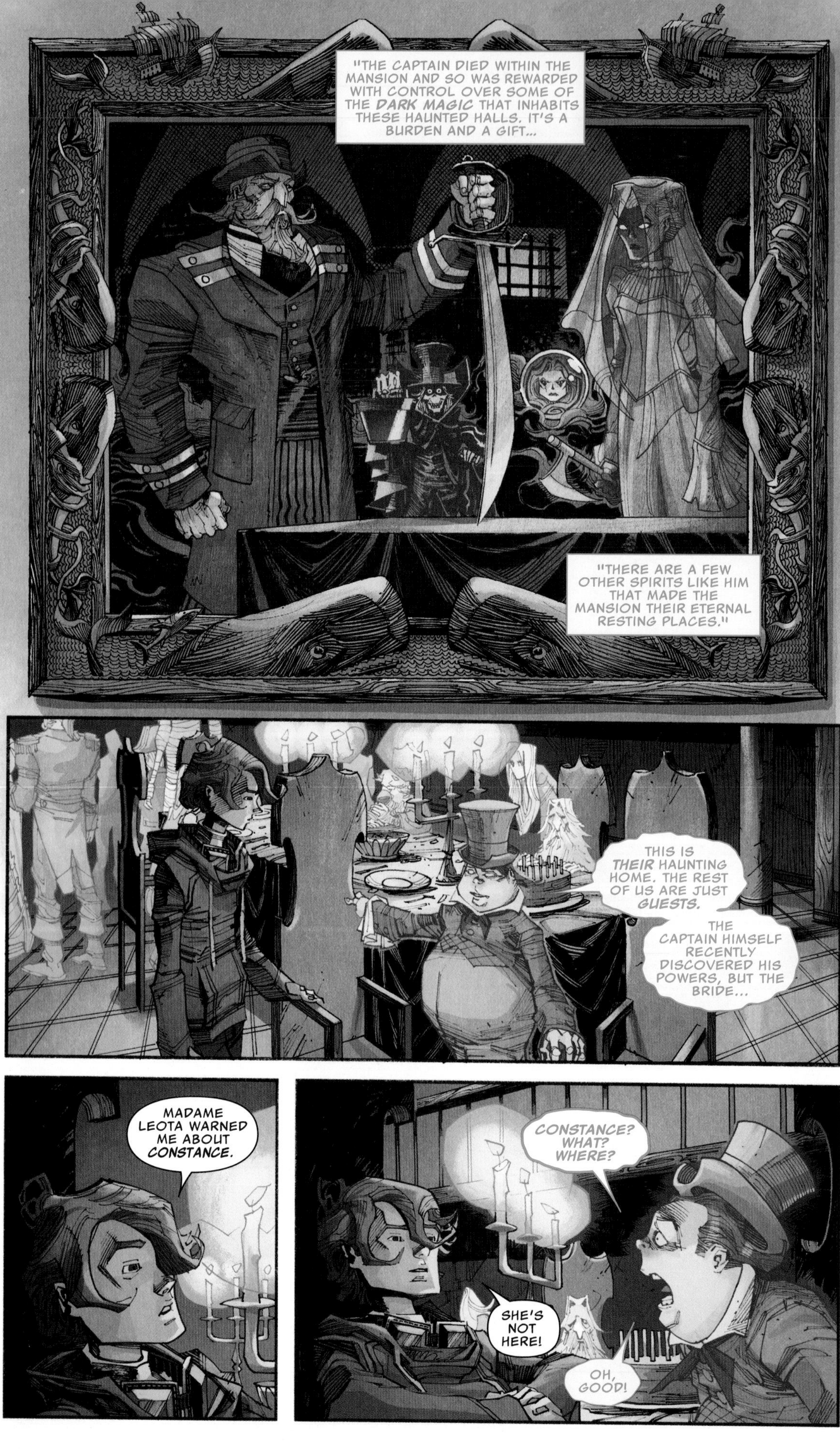
"THE CAPTAIN DIED WITHIN THE MANSION AND SO WAS REWARDED WITH CONTROL OVER SOME OF THE DARK MAGIC THAT INHABITS THESE HAUNTED HALLS. IT'S A BURDEN AND A GIFT...
"THERE ARE A FEW OTHER SPIRITS LIKE HIM THAT MADE THE MANSION THEIR ETERNAL RESTING PLACES."
THIS IS THEIR HAUNTING HOME. THE REST OF US ARE JUST GUESTS.
THE CAPTAIN HIMSELF RECENTLY DISCOVERED HIS POWERS, BUT THE BRIDE...
MADAME LEOTA WARNED ME ABOUT CONSTANCE.
CONSTANCE? WHAT? WHERE?
SHE'S NOT HERE!
OH, GOOD!

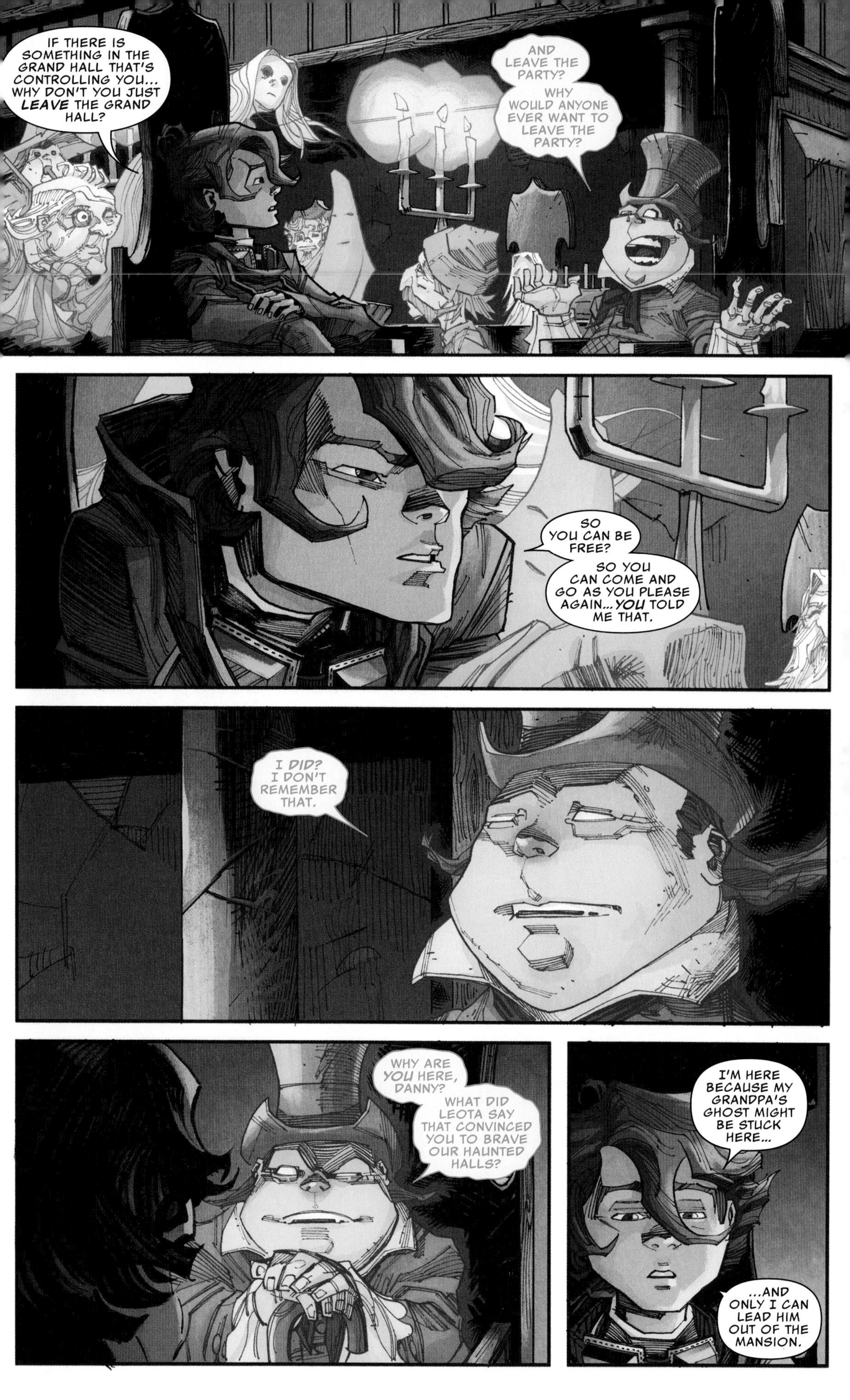
IF THERE IS SOMETHING IN THE GRAND HALL THAT'S CONTROLLING YOU... WHY DON'T YOU JUST LEAVE THE GRAND HALL?
AND LEAVE THE PARTY?
WHY WOULD ANYONE EVER WANT TO LEAVE THE PARTY?
SO YOU CAN BE FREE?
SO YOU CAN COME AND GO AS YOU PLEASE AGAIN...YOU TOLD ME THAT.
I DID? I DON'T REMEMBER THAT.
WHY ARE YOU HERE, DANNY?
WHAT DID LEOTA SAY THAT CONVINCED YOU TO BRAVE OUR HAUNTED HALLS?
I'M HERE BECAUSE MY GRANDPA'S GHOST MIGHT BE STUCK HERE...
...AND ONLY I CAN LEAD HIM OUT OF THE MANSION.

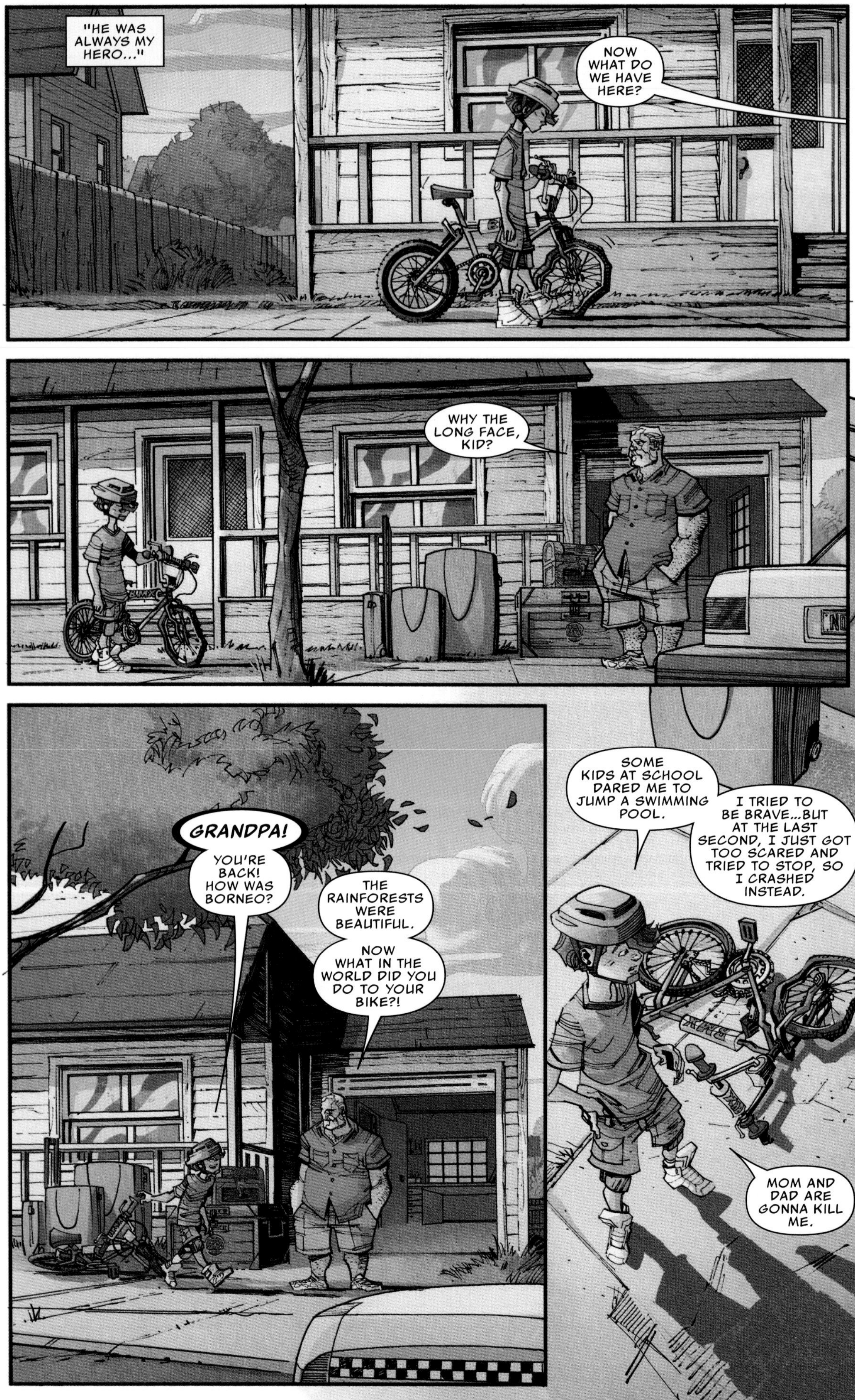
"HE WAS ALWAYS MY HERO..."
NOW WHAT DO WE HAVE HERE?
WHY THE LONG FACE, KID?
GRANDPA!
YOU'RE BACK! HOW WAS BORNEO?
THE RAINFORESTS WERE BEAUTIFUL.
NOW WHAT IN THE WORLD DID YOU DO TO YOUR BIKE?!
SOME KIDS AT SCHOOL DARED ME TO JUMP A SWIMMING POOL.
I TRIED TO BE BRAVE...BUT AT THE LAST SECOND, I JUST GOT TOO SCARED AND TRIED TO STOP, SO I CRASHED INSTEAD.
MOM AND DAD ARE GONNA KILL ME.

AT LEAST YOU CONSIDERED IT. A LOT OF PEOPLE WOULDN'T HAVE EVEN GOTTEN ON THE BIKE.

BUT I STILL CRASHED...

I'VE TAKEN A FEW FALLS MYSELF, DANNY. IT HAPPENS.

WHAT MATTERS IS IF YOU GET BACK UP AND TRY AGAIN.

YOUR GRANDMOTHER TAUGHT ME THAT.

DO...DO YOU MISS HER?

DEARLY...

SOMEDAY I WILL FIND HER AGAIN.

IS THAT WHY YOU TRAVEL THE WORLD SO MUCH? YOU'RE LOOKING FOR HER GHOST?

SOMETHING LIKE THAT...

YOU SHOULD BE HANGING OUT WITH KIDS YOUR OWN AGE.

BUT LISTEN TO ME, GOING ON LIKE SOME OLD FART.

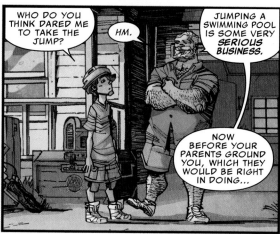

WHO DO YOU THINK DARED ME TO TAKE THE JUMP?

HM.

JUMPING A SWIMMING POOL IS SOME VERY SERIOUS BUSINESS.

NOW BEFORE YOUR PARENTS GROUND YOU, WHICH THEY WOULD BE RIGHT IN DOING...

...CAN I TELL YOU A SECRET?

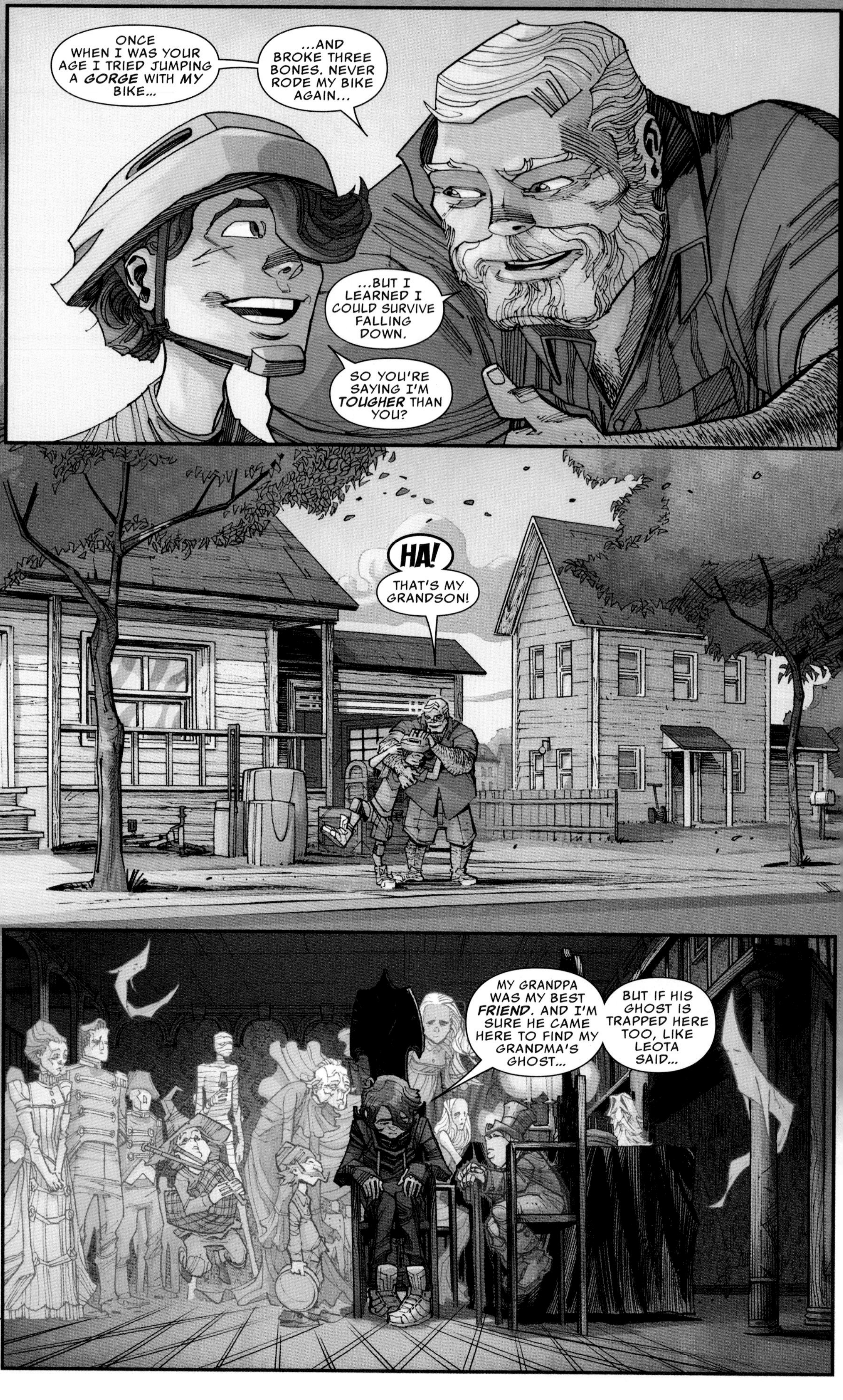
ONCE WHEN I WAS YOUR AGE I TRIED JUMPING A GORGE WITH MY BIKE...
...AND BROKE THREE BONES. NEVER RODE MY BIKE AGAIN...
...BUT I LEARNED I COULD SURVIVE FALLING DOWN.
SO YOU'RE SAYING I'M TOUGHER THAN YOU?
HA!
THAT'S MY GRANDSON!
MY GRANDPA WAS MY BEST FRIEND. AND I'M SURE HE CAME HERE TO FIND MY GRANDMA'S GHOST...
BUT IF HIS GHOST IS TRAPPED HERE TOO, LIKE LEOTA SAID...

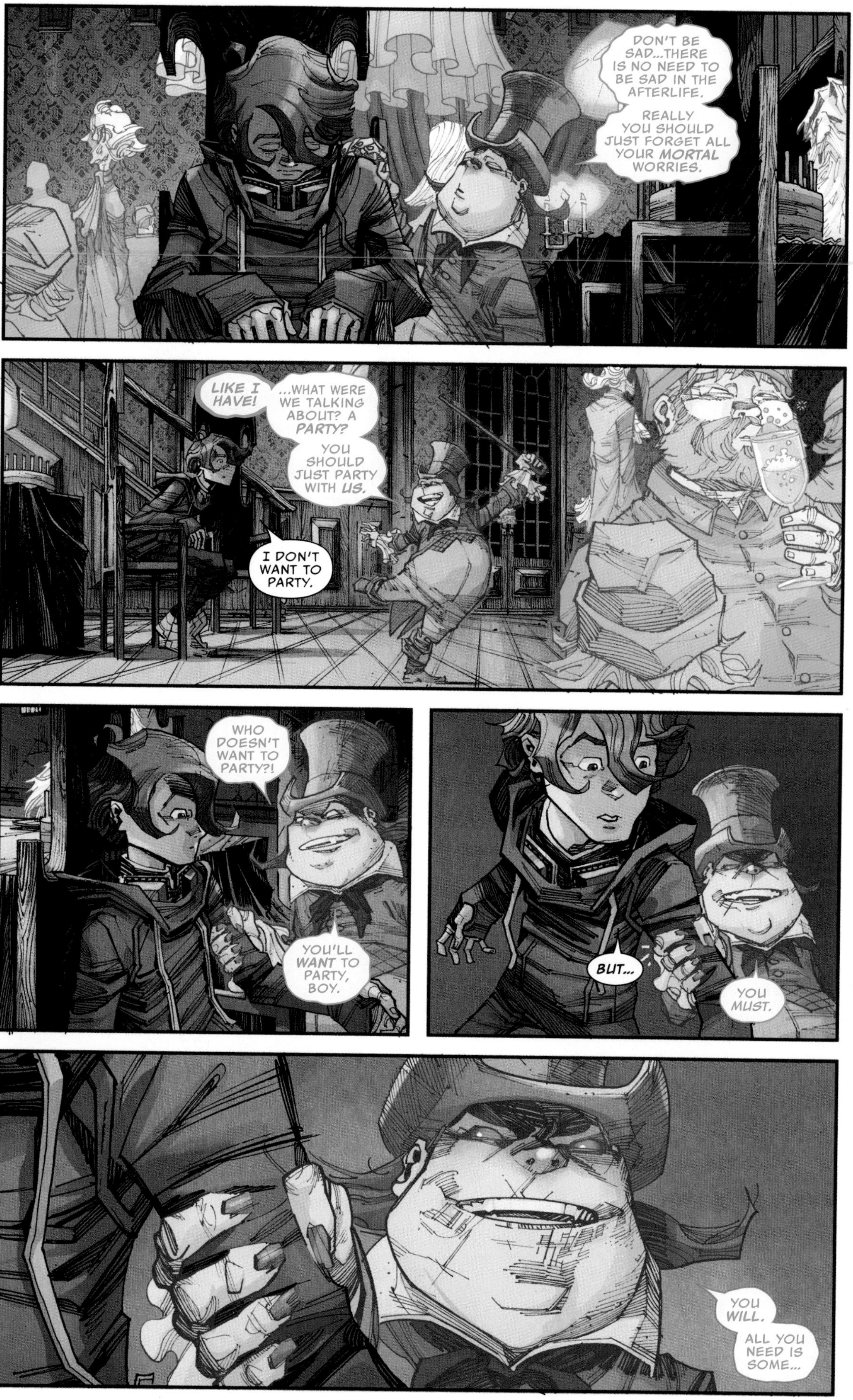
DON'T BE SAD...THERE IS NO NEED TO BE SAD IN THE AFTERLIFE.
REALLY YOU SHOULD JUST FORGET ALL YOUR MORTAL WORRIES.
LIKE I HAVE!
...WHAT WERE WE TALKING ABOUT? A PARTY?
YOU SHOULD JUST PARTY WITH US.
I DON'T WANT TO PARTY.
WHO DOESN'T WANT TO PARTY?!
YOU'LL WANT TO PARTY, BOY.
BUT...
YOU MUST.
YOU WILL.
ALL YOU NEED IS SOME...

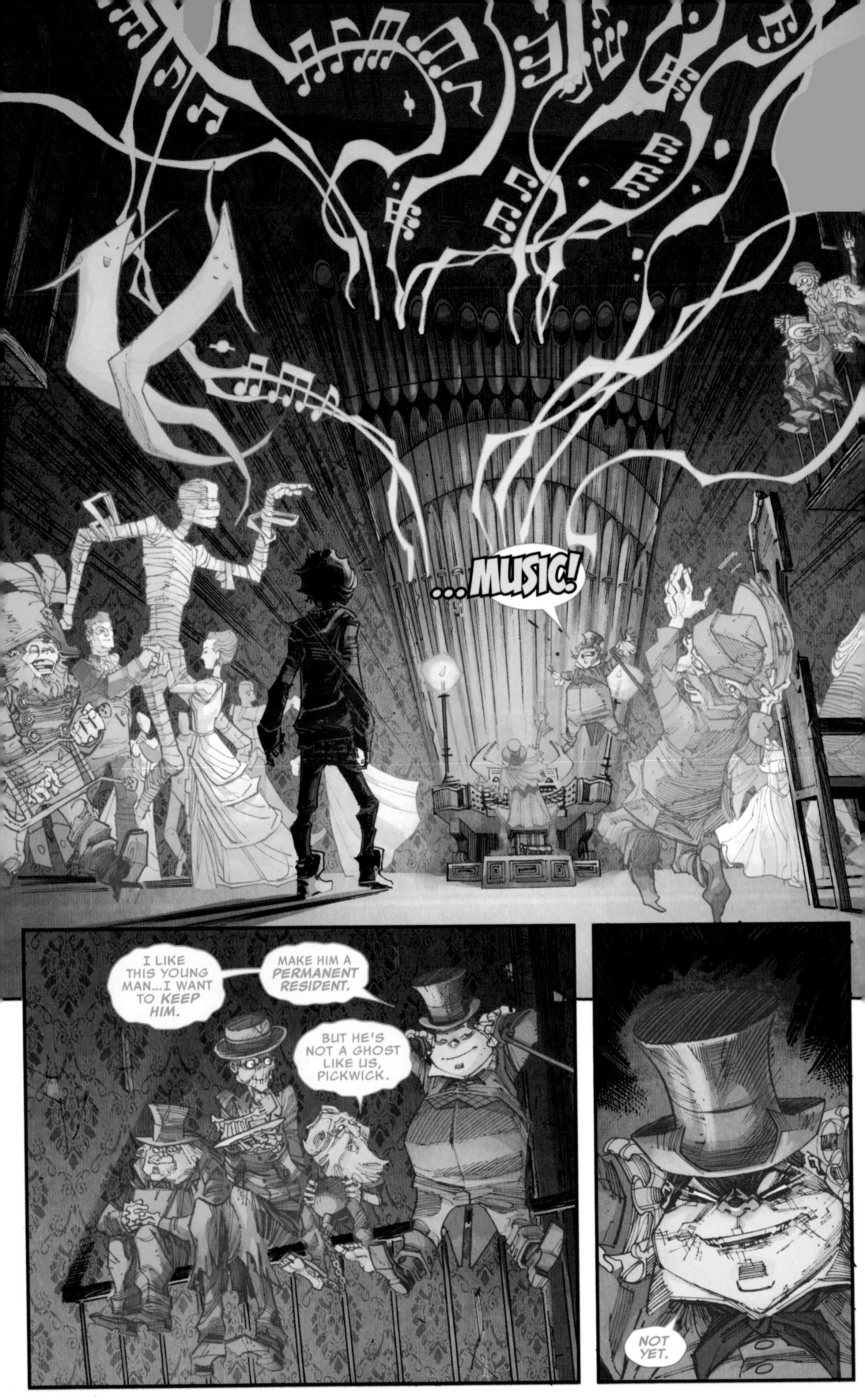

...MUSIC!
I LIKE THIS YOUNG MAN...I WANT TO KEEP HIM.
MAKE HIM A PERMANENT RESIDENT.
BUT HE'S NOT A GHOST LIKE US, PICKWICK.
NOT YET.

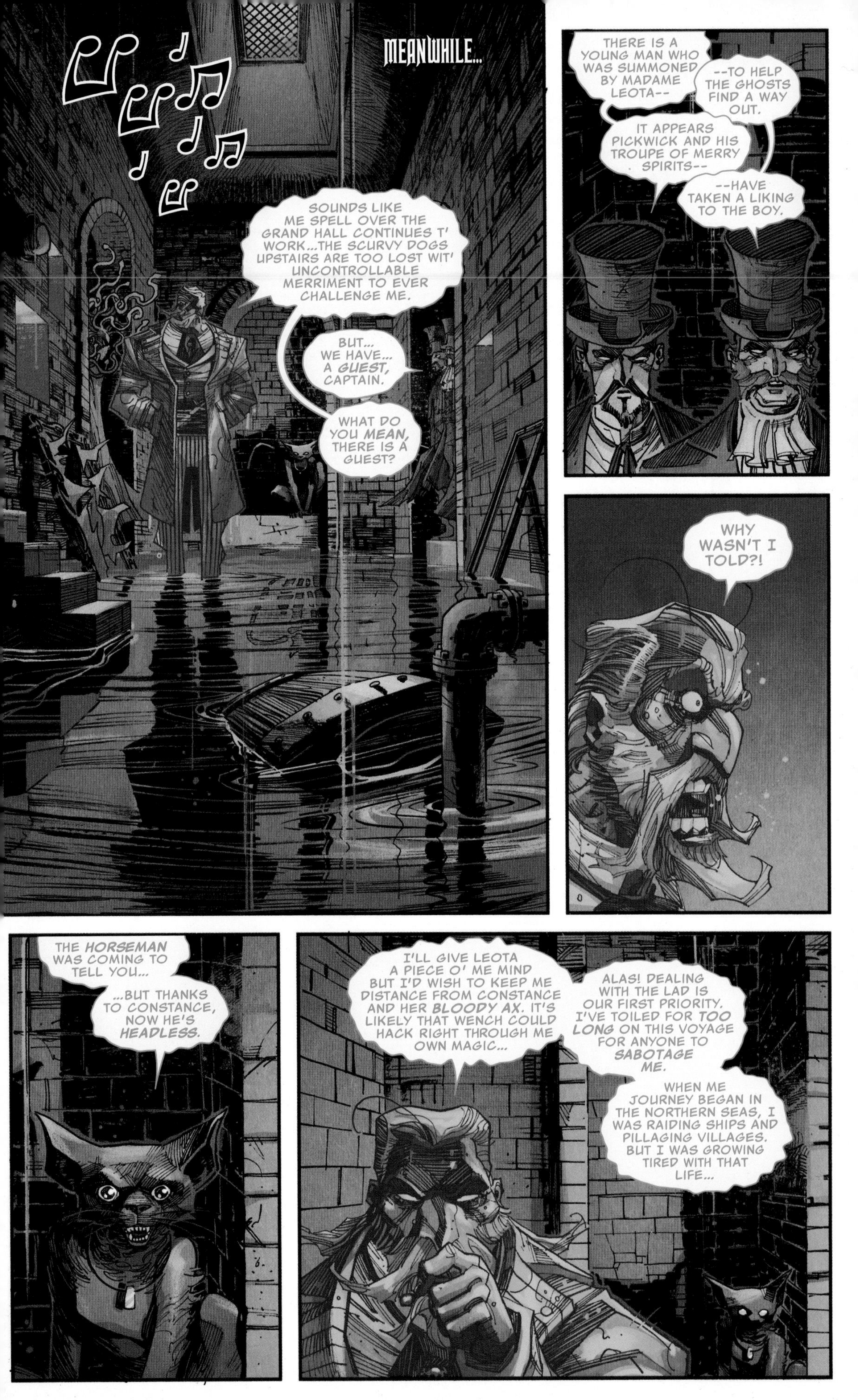
MEANWHILE...
SOUNDS LIKE ME SPELL OVER THE GRAND HALL CONTINUES T' WORK...THE SCURVY DOGS UPSTAIRS ARE TOO LOST WIT' UNCONTROLLABLE MERRIMENT TO EVER CHALLENGE ME.
BUT... WE HAVE... A GUEST, CAPTAIN.
WHAT DO YOU MEAN, THERE IS A GUEST?
THERE IS A YOUNG MAN WHO WAS SUMMONED BY MADAME LEOTA--
--TO HELP THE GHOSTS FIND A WAY OUT.
IT APPEARS PICKWICK AND HIS TROUPE OF MERRY SPIRITS--
--HAVE TAKEN A LIKING TO THE BOY.
WHY WASN'T I TOLD?!
THE HORSEMAN WAS COMING TO TELL YOU...
...BUT THANKS TO CONSTANCE, NOW HE'S HEADLESS.
I'LL GIVE LEOTA A PIECE O' ME MIND BUT I'D WISH TO KEEP ME DISTANCE FROM CONSTANCE AND HER BLOODY AX. IT'S LIKELY THAT WENCH COULD HACK RIGHT THROUGH ME OWN MAGIC...
ALAS! DEALING WITH THE LAD IS OUR FIRST PRIORITY. I'VE TOILED FOR TOO LONG ON THIS VOYAGE FOR ANYONE TO SABOTAGE ME.
WHEN ME JOURNEY BEGAN IN THE NORTHERN SEAS, I WAS RAIDING SHIPS AND PILLAGING VILLAGES. BUT I WAS GROWING TIRED WITH THAT LIFE...

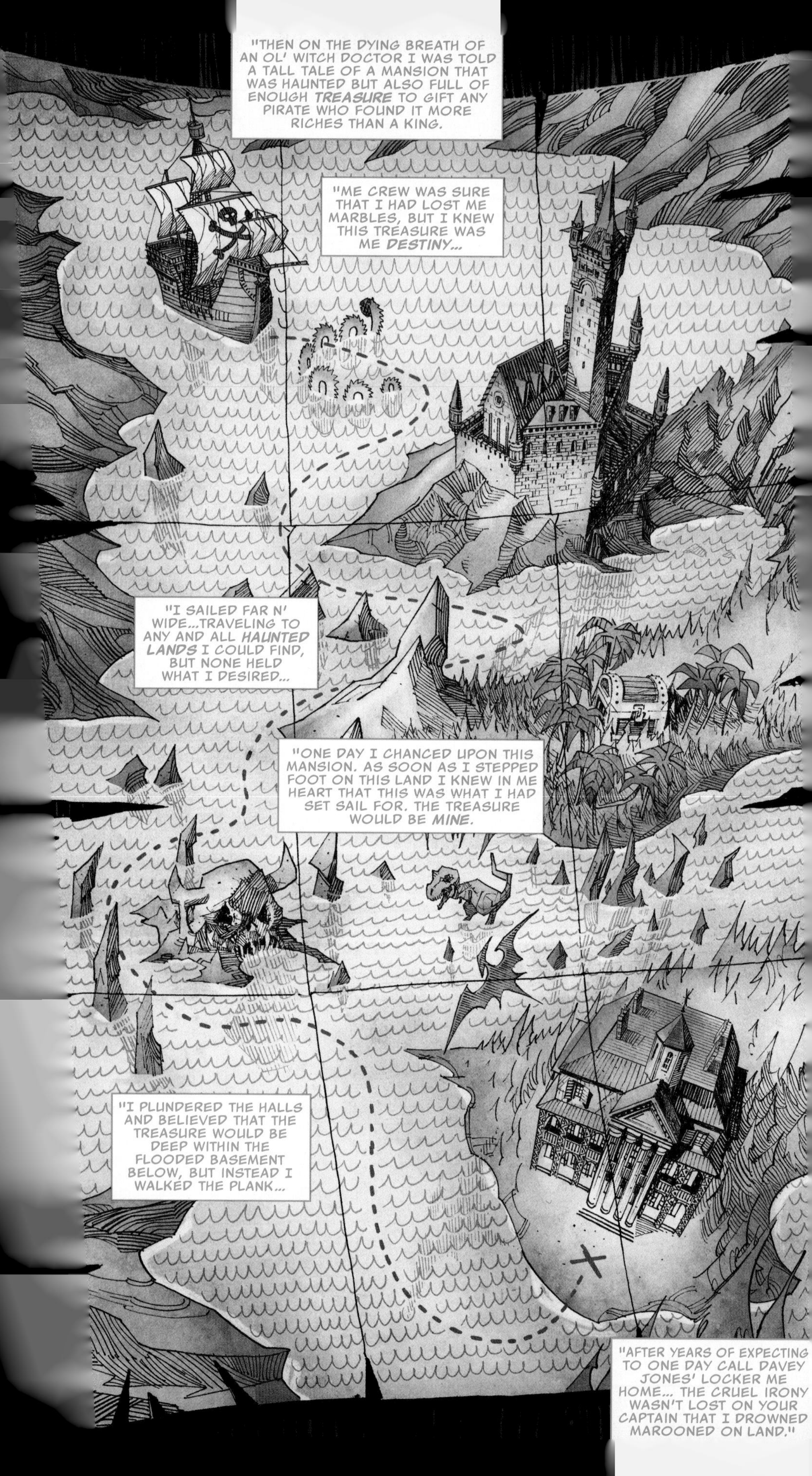
"THEN ON THE DYING BREATH OF AN OL' WITCH DOCTOR I WAS TOLD A TALL TALE OF A MANSION THAT WAS HAUNTED BUT ALSO FULL OF ENOUGH TREASURE TO GIFT ANY PIRATE WHO FOUND IT MORE RICHES THAN A KING.
"ME CREW WAS SURE THAT I HAD LOST ME MARBLES, BUT I KNEW THIS TREASURE WAS ME DESTINY...
"I SAILED FAR N' WIDE...TRAVELING TO ANY AND ALL HAUNTED LANDS I COULD FIND, BUT NONE HELD WHAT I DESIRED...
"ONE DAY I CHANCED UPON THIS MANSION. AS SOON AS I STEPPED FOOT ON THIS LAND I KNEW IN ME HEART THAT THIS WAS WHAT I HAD SET SAIL FOR. THE TREASURE WOULD BE MINE.
"I PLUNDERED THE HALLS AND BELIEVED THAT THE TREASURE WOULD BE DEEP WITHIN THE FLOODED BASEMENT BELOW, BUT INSTEAD I WALKED THE PLANK...
"AFTER YEARS OF EXPECTING TO ONE DAY CALL DAVEY JONES' LOCKER ME HOME... THE CRUEL IRONY WASN'T LOST ON YOUR CAPTAIN THAT I DROWNED MAROONED ON LAND."

MY SPIRIT SHOULD BE THE SCOURGE OF THE SEVEN SEAS!

ALL THE OTHER GHOSTS WERE ALWAYS ALLOWED TO SET SAIL AS THEY PLEASED, BUT BECAUSE I LOST ME LIFE IN THE MANSION I'M *TRAPPED!*

ME SEARCH FOR THE TREASURE IS THE ONLY THING KEEPING MY DARK SOUL TIED TO THIS REALM!

THE CURSE I PLACED ON THE GRAND HALL WILL MAKE THOSE SCALLYWAGS FEEL MY PAIN WHILE I FIND THE TREASURE IN THE MANSION...

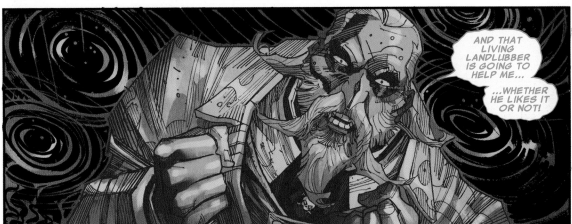

AND THAT LIVING LANDLUBBER IS GOING TO HELP ME...

...WHETHER HE LIKES IT OR NOT!

HEY...I CAN'T...

SLOW DOWN!

SHOULDN'T WE BE TRYING TO GET YOU FREE?!

OH, COME NOW. THERE'S NO REASON TO BE A PARTY POOPER.

YOU'RE HARDLY EVEN TRYING TO ENJOY YOURSELF.

BUT...

IF YOU TRY... *REALLY TRY*...TO HAVE FUN HERE, I PROMISE THAT WE WILL HELP YOU WITH... WHATEVER IT IS THAT YOU SAID YOU NEED TO DO.

DEAL?

OKAY... MAYBE FOR A MINUTE...

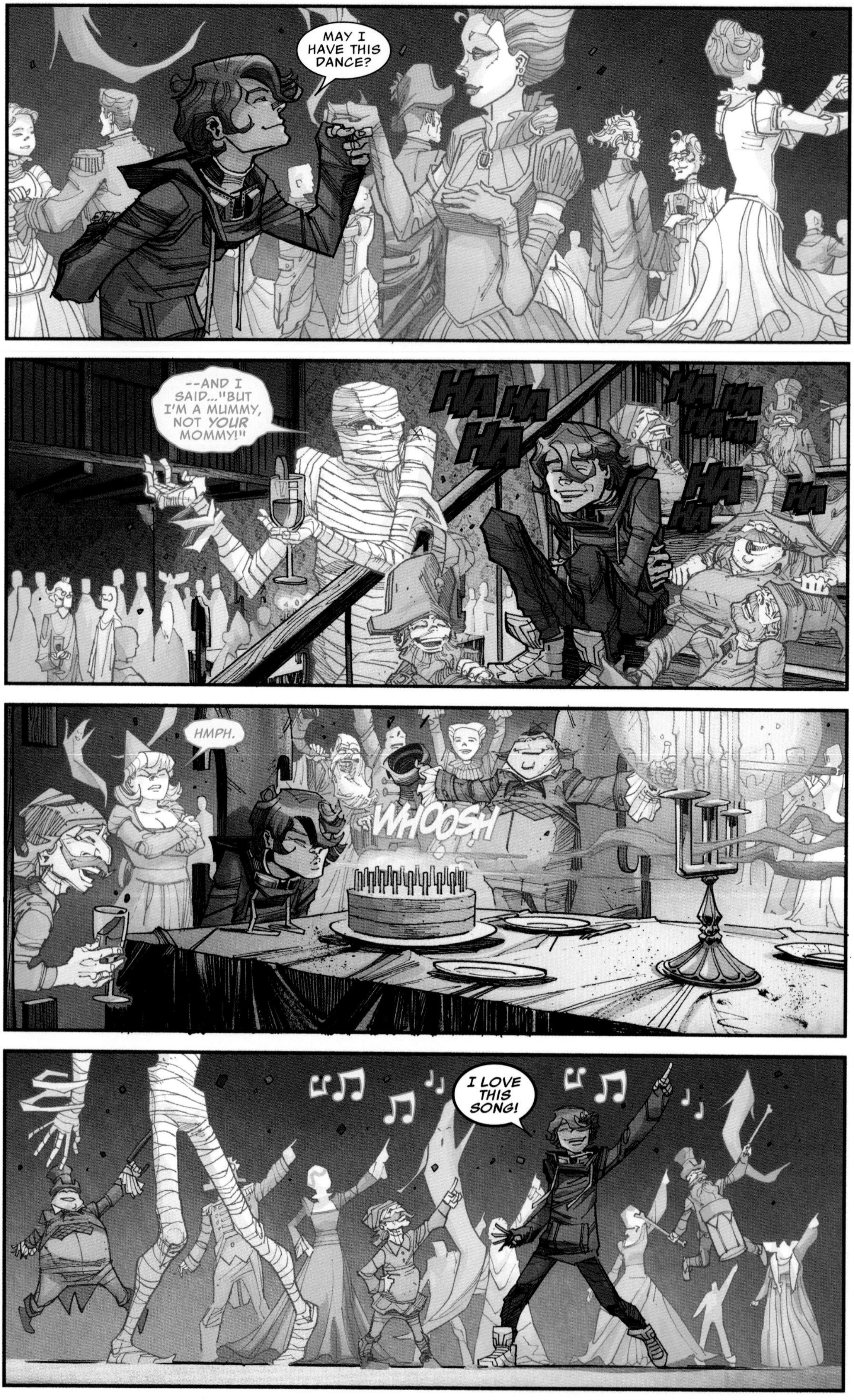
MAY I HAVE THIS DANCE?
--AND I SAID..."BUT I'M A MUMMY, NOT YOUR MOMMY!"
HA HA HA
HA HA HA HA
HA HA
HA
HMPH.
WHOOSH
I LOVE THIS SONG!

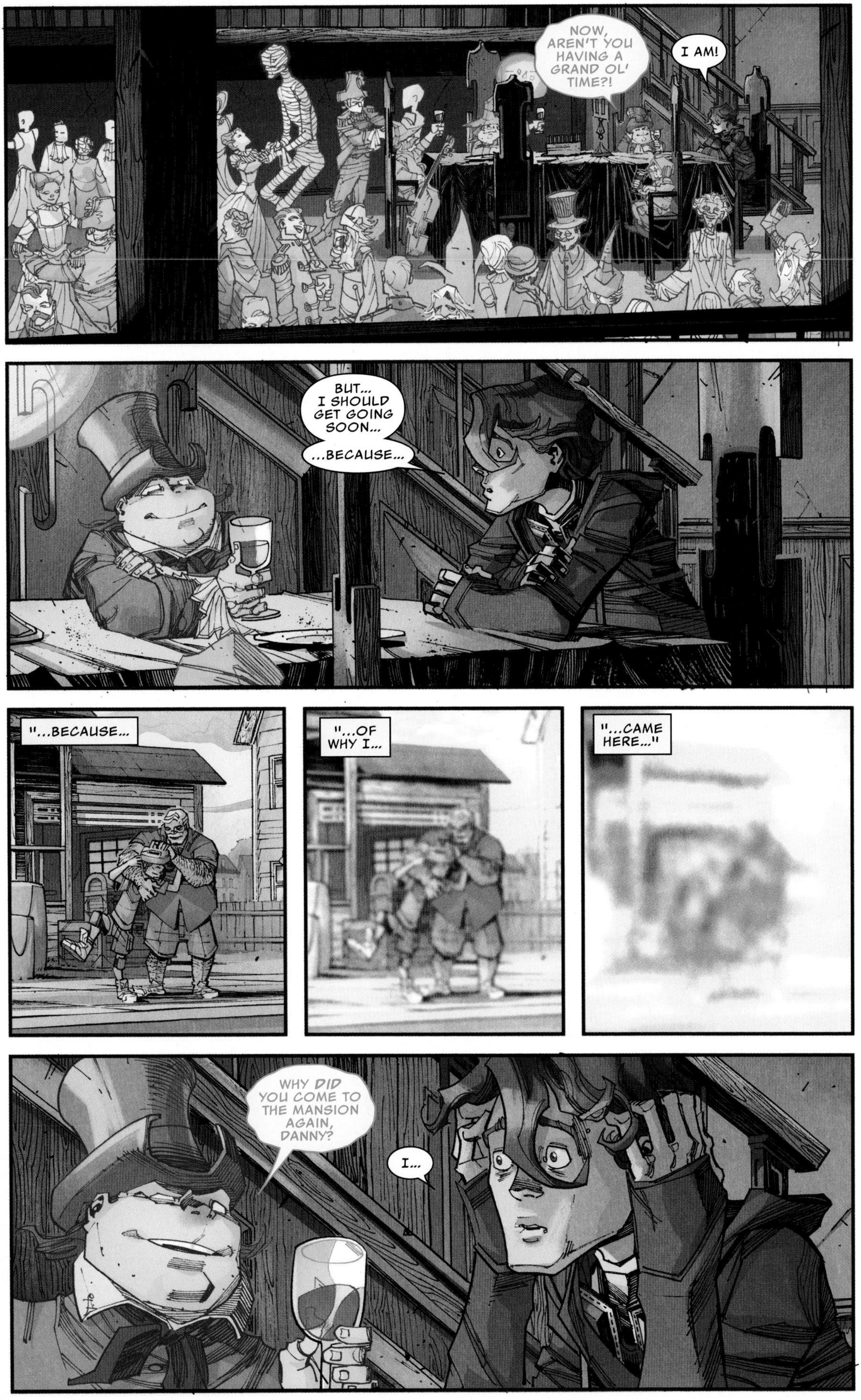
NOW, AREN'T YOU HAVING A GRAND OL' TIME?!
I AM!
BUT... I SHOULD GET GOING SOON...
...BECAUSE...
"...BECAUSE...
"...OF WHY I...
"...CAME HERE..."
WHY DID YOU COME TO THE MANSION AGAIN, DANNY?
I...

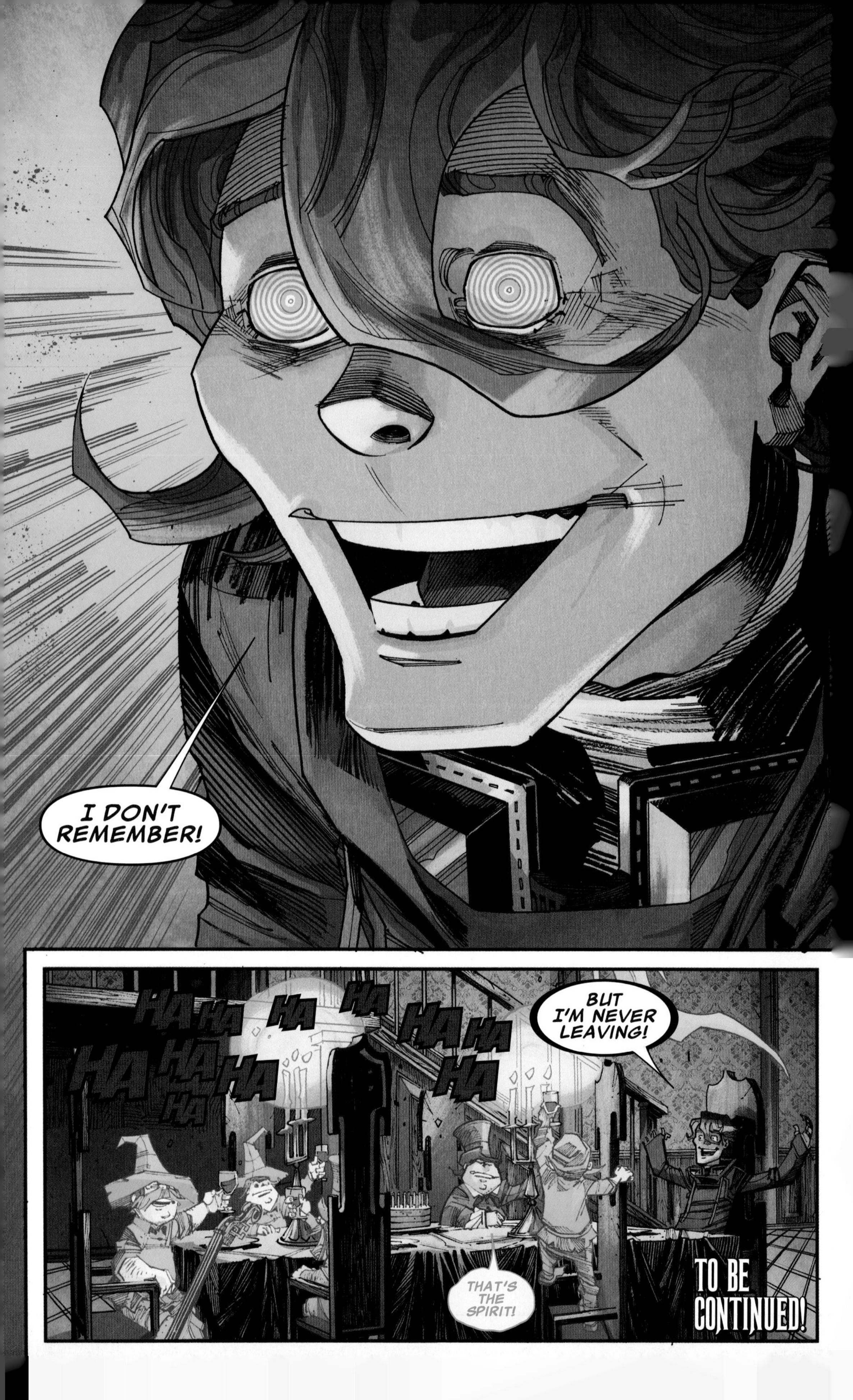
I DON'T REMEMBER!
HA HA HA HA HA HA HA HA HA HA HA HA HA
BUT I'M NEVER LEAVING!
THAT'S THE SPIRIT!
TO BE CONTINUED!

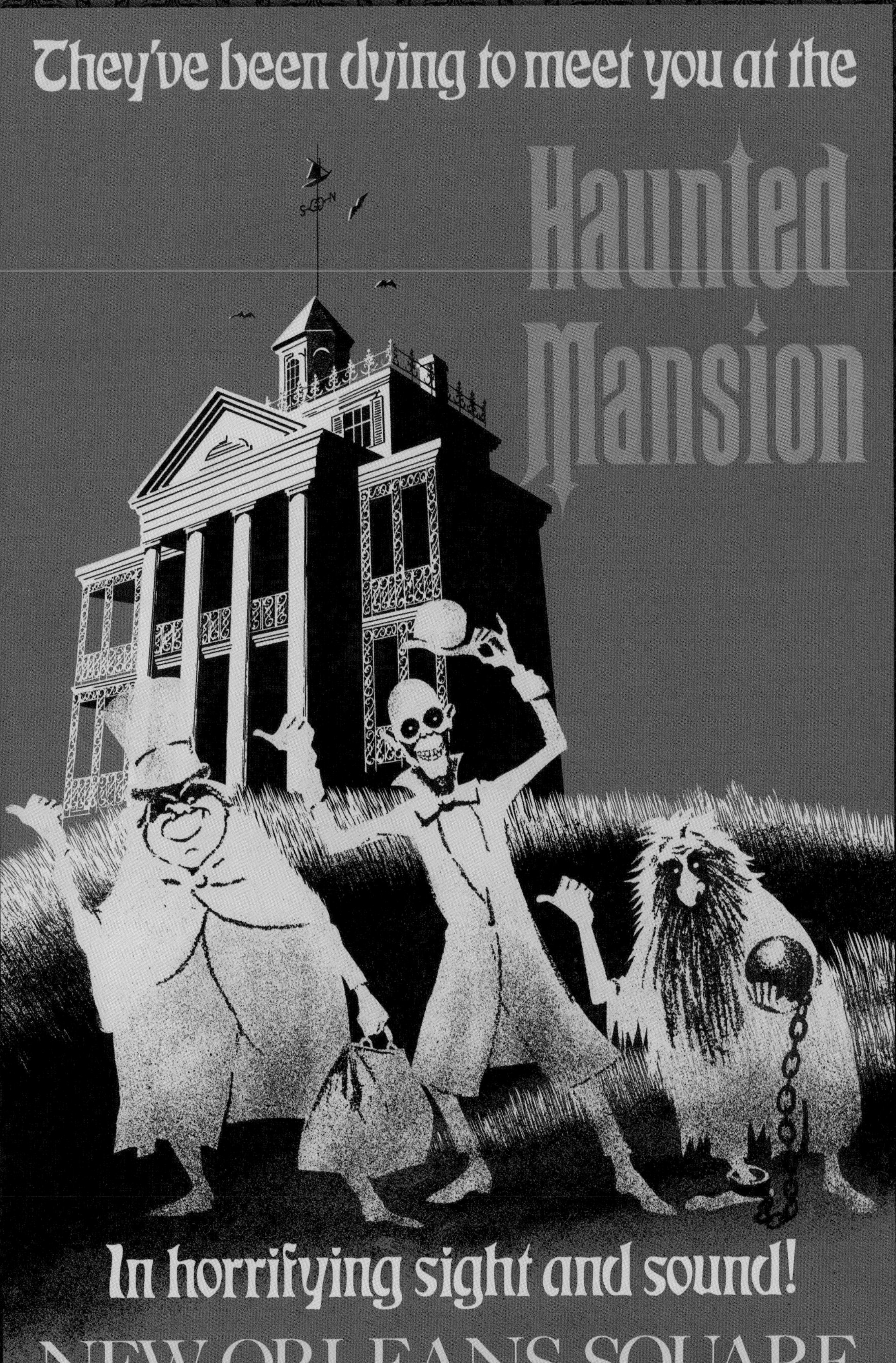
They've been dying to meet you at the
Haunted Mansion
In horrifying sight and sound!
NEW ORLEANS SQUARE
© WALT DISNEY PRODUCTIONS

No. 2 Disney Parks Variant by **Ken Chapman & Marc Davis**.
Image courtesy of the Walt Disney Archives.

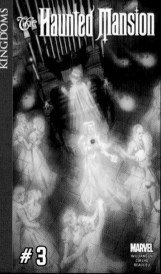